"Dodger Dog Visits the Air Ambulance"

Written by Karen Gee

Illustrations by Kim Wymer

ISBN: 9798665685304

Thank you so much for buying this book, which is number eleven in the Dodger Dog series.

'Dodger Dog Visits the Air Ambulance' is designed to teach children about Accident and Trauma!
In Dodger's work as a Pet Therapy Dog, he regularly visits the Trauma Centre where patients are being treated following a serious incident.

Dodger visits the helicopter where he learns how the Air Ambulance Service saves lives at the accident scene and how the crew make a big difference to the health of the people they meet.

Find out all about Dodger's mission to help others on his website www.dodgerdog.co.uk

You can also follow Dodger Dog's adventures on Instagram, Facebook, and Twitter @Ilovedodgerdog

Every Dodger Dog book purchased means that you are helping an animal rescue charity, either in the UK or across the world.

The details of some of the charities Dodger Dog supports are available on his website www.dodgerdog.co.uk

ACKNOWLEDGEMENTS

Karen – My inspiration comes from my love of dogs and passion for helping others. From an early age, dogs were a big part of my life. I passionately believe that every dog deserves to be loved and cherished.

Kim – I was, initially, a cat person. I started painting cats and was a cat owner for many years, until I met Dodger, fell in love with him, and my love of dogs began.

We would both like to thank our families for their love and support. A special thank you to Sinead for her help with getting yet another Dodger Dog into print, and Siobhan for originally bringing Dodger into our lives. We would also like to give a massive thank you to the amazing Dodger Dog Team. You can meet them all on our website www.dodgerdog.co.uk

Dodger Dog Visits the Air Ambulance

It was a sunny Tuesday morning and Dodger was sitting patiently on the platform waiting for the tube train to arrive. He was wearing his bright yellow Pet Therapy jacket and he knew that this could only mean one thing! He was going to see the patients at the big hospital in London somewhere Dodger loves to visit.

Dodger loves to travel on trains and tubes, and when he wears his beautiful yellow therapy jacket, he gets lots of strokes and attention. This makes Dodgers tail wag extremely fast, also it makes Dodger smile a very big Staffie smile, which always brightens up the day for everyone sitting in the train carriage with him.

As the train doors opened, mummy said to Dodger, "Here we are, this is our stop." Dodger stood next to mummy and walked slowly and carefully onto the platform, making sure that he listened carefully to mummy's instructions, especially the one to "mind the gap". He did not want any accidents to happen on his way to the hospital.

When they arrived at the hospital entrance, Dodger knew
exactly where he was going. As he walked in through the
big glass doors, he was excited and happy, especially as
Dodger's first stop was always to see his friends in the Air
Ambulance Charity Shop. Dodger really did like all of the
lovely volunteers who worked there.

Dodger ran into the shop wagging his tail excitedly, saying good morning to everyone inside! The shop was such an important place as it raises much needed funds to support the Air Ambulance Service. Dodger looked around at all the pictures and models of the big red air ambulance and wondered what it was like to go inside.

"Time to go upstairs now, Dodger," mummy said, "all of the patients on the ward will be waiting to see you."
Dodger turned around and waved goodbye, smiling to himself, still wondering what it would be like to be inside the big beautiful red helicopter?

"Where are we going first?" Dodger asked as they headed towards the lift. As Dodger walked through the lift doors he knew immediately, and his question was answered. The lift that they were using was incredibly special, and it was the one that would take them to the trauma unit, and it was also used by the Air Ambulance crew.

Dodger always hoped that on his visits to the trauma unit, he would see the helicopter crew. But he knew that they worked with serious emergencies and maybe a little dog could be in their way as they rushed their patients to get the help that they needed quickly! Still Dodger thought it would be extremely exciting to help save lives.

As Dodger walked towards the entrance to the ward, he thought about how important it was to visit the patients here. They really needed love and kindness to support them with their recovery after a serious injury, which can be really life changing as a result. Dodger knew that the Air Ambulance and its crew just like him were on a mission.

The Air Ambulance mission was "to save more lives through rapid response and cutting-edge care." Just like Dodger, they had values. They were compassionate, they really care about people, courageous, brave, work in challenging and difficult situations, also pioneering, leading with change and new ways to help others.

Dodger greeted the doctors and nurses on the ward first, and then mummy asked who they thought would benefit from a visit from Dodger? The ward sister straight away smiled and told them about a patient who was missing their own dog. 'Great!' thought Dodger, as he headed to the bed. 'Some lovely cuddles are on the way to them.'

As he walked towards the bed, Dodger saw a young boy with his leg in a big plaster cast, raised up in the air in front of him! Dodger ran over and jumped on the big plastic chair beside the bed. "Hello, my name is Dodger" he barked "What is your name?" The boy looked up at Dodger and replied, "Hi Dodger, my name is Peter".

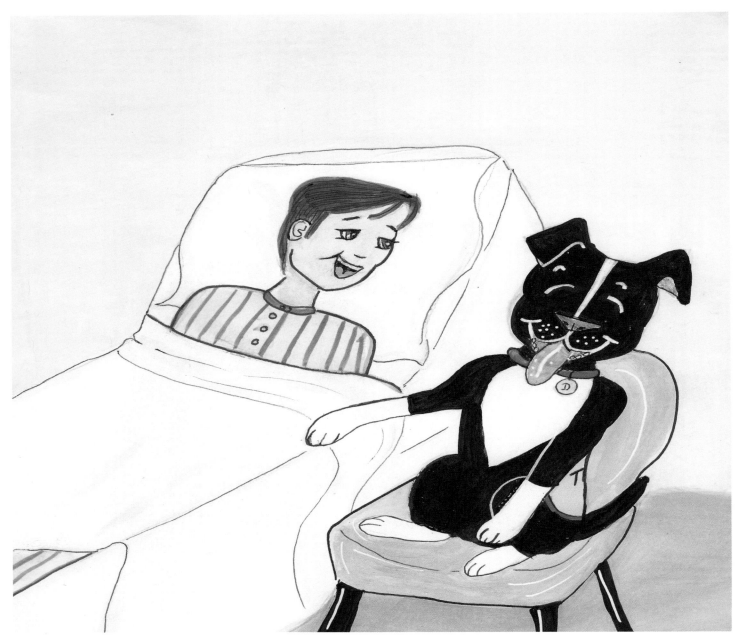

Peter seemed incredibly surprised to see Dodger sitting there at his bed side, and asked, "What are you doing here Dodger? It's really nice to meet you." Dodger smiled a big Staffie smile back at Peter and whoofed! "I am a Pet Therapy dog, Peter, and I visit this ward regularly to spend time with patients just like you!"

"What happened to your leg?" Dodger asked. Peter reached out his hand and gently began stroking Dodgers fur, he replied, "I fell off of my bike and was hit by a car." Dodger was very shocked "Oh no!" he gasped, "I'm sorry to hear that. You are in the right place now to get better quickly. This is a fabulous hospital and the staff are great."

Peter smiled "yes, I know, the treatment I have received since my accident has been amazing, from the moment the helicopter arrived!" At that, Dodger's ears pricked up. He sat up straight and barked "Oh Peter! please tell me more! I would love to see and experience what it is like inside the beautiful Air Ambulance helicopter one day."

Peter was surprised to hear Dodger say this and wondered if he fully understood what the helicopter was used for? He decided that it might be a good idea to explain its work to him. "Oh Dodger, I know that it looks exciting, but really you would have to have had a serious injury to be treated by the Air Ambulance team which is quite scary.

"They are only sent out after an emergency call is made to request an ambulance, when there has been a very serious injury." Dodger was shocked and said, "So you must have had a really traumatic experience and been very ill Peter? I am so pleased that you received the help that you needed at the roadside. Please tell me more."

Peter smiled and continued his story. "My accident was very serious indeed, I needed specialist treatment very quickly, in order to save my life." Dodger was listening very carefully to his story. "The Air Ambulance has a team of specialist doctors on board who can do procedures and give treatment, not given by other ambulance crews."

Dodger was interested and impressed by Peter's story. "I did break my leg quite badly in the accident," Peter told Dodger. "Also, I lost a large amount of blood, and my heart was beating extremely fast, which was dangerous. That's the reason the Air Ambulance came to help me. I was lucky this type of help was available."

"Wow you are very brave Peter" barked Dodger.
Peter thanked Dodger for his kindness, then responded "The
Air Ambulance team are the brave ones, they save lives.
That is really something special, an amazing thing to do.
They save lives every single day and night of the year."

Dodger agreed, "It was not the best situation to fly for the first time in a helicopter," Peter laughed, "I didn't fly in the helicopter Dodger, they treated me and when it was safe, they drove me here." This did surprise Dodger. "I don't understand why, when they have a helicopter?"

Peter explained that, "Out of 100 people treated by the Air Ambulance, only 20 get taken to hospital by helicopter, sometimes the ground is quicker than the air." Dodger then asked, "What if you need a doctor on your journey?" "No problem, the medics come in the Ambulance." Peter replied.

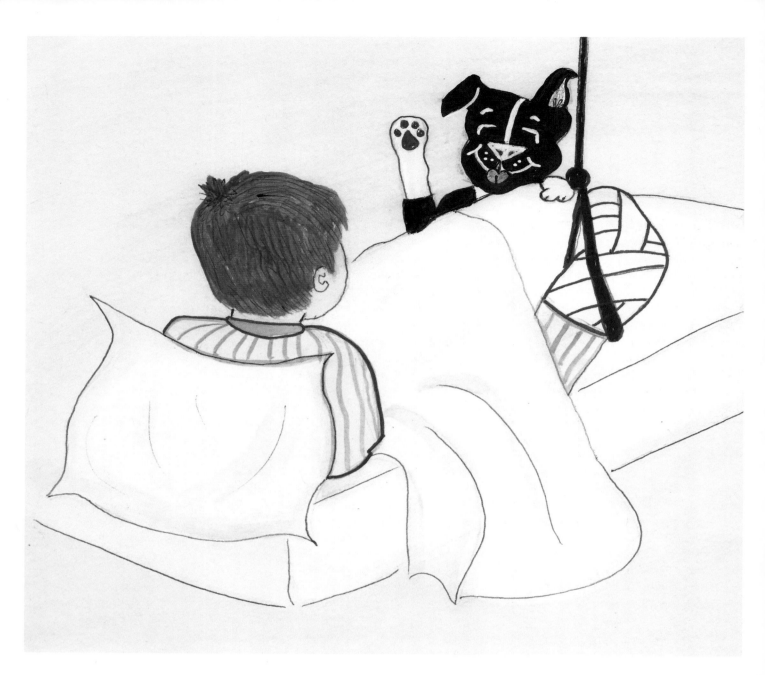

Dodger thanked Peter for sharing what was a scary experience. Peter then thanked Dodger for listening, "It really helps to talk, and talking to you has been great, thank you for listening." Dodger wagged his tail 'Goodbye.' Mummy cleaned the chair he had sat on before they left.

In the next bed sat a young girl with a large bandage around her head and a big foam collar around her neck. As Dodger walked over, the young girl smiled and said, "Hello doggie," to Dodger. With that Dodger asked, "What has happened to you?" The young girl started to tell her story. "I fell out of a big tree," she explained.

Dodger knew climbing trees was dangerous. As he listened, he decided to keep his paws firmly on the ground. The young girl told him her name was Avni, she had 3 brothers who also all liked to climb trees. Avni said she was the best climber and that day she had climbed the highest!

Suddenly Avni lost her footing she fell hitting her head on the way down. "What happened next?" Dodger asked. Avni did not remember, her family called for an Ambulance and very quickly the Air Ambulance arrived. She was treated at the scene and then flown to hospital by helicopter.

Hearing the two stories Dodger was starting to understand how the Air Ambulance works, and its important job. Avni explained the journey by road would have taken too long, so it was decided she should be transported by helicopter to get her to the trauma centre as quickly as possible.

Avni thanked Dodger for his visit saying that talking had
really helped her today. Dodger walked away feeling proud
that he had been kind and thoughtful and helped others. As
Dodger prepared to leave the ward, he saw a group of
Doctors talking. Much to his surprise, they were wearing
familiar red jumpsuits!

Dodgers tail began to wag fast, they were Air Ambulance crew. They saw Dodger, "Hey, look at the Pet Therapy dog! What's your name buddy?" Dodger ran towards them barking loudly, "My name is Dodger, really pleased to meet you. I have been talking to 2 of your patients, Peter and Avni and they told me all about the work that you do."

They knew about Dodger's work, suddenly one of the Doctors asked, "Hey Dodger, how would you like to see our Air Ambulance for yourself?" Dodger jumped up and down excitedly barking, "YES, PLEASE!" "Come on then Dodger," they replied, "Follow us". One extremely excited Dodger followed them into the incredibly special helicopter pad lift!"

At the top, the lift doors opened what a sight it was to see!
Mummy held Dodger's lead as they followed behind
walking slowly up the sloping platform to the big red
helicopter. The helipad was at the very top of the hospital
on the roof, and the view of the city was totally breath-
taking. Dodger stared wide eyed at the tall buildings.

As they approached the take-off pad, Dodger could see the magnificent big red helicopter waiting there, ready for action. "Would you like to climb inside?" the doctor asked Dodger, "yes please," he replied, "I would love that, thank you." Dodger sat in the side door, he also climbed on one of the crew seats and he tried on one of the helmets.

Dodger was grateful for this opportunity and pleased that the Air Ambulance was available to help people and to save lives. "I wish Peter and Avni could see this now." Dodger barked, the doctor smiled and said, "when patients are fully recovered, they are able to visit the helicopter up here just like you have today Dodger."

"That is pawsome news!" barked Dodger. "they will look forward to that." Dodger thanked the helicopter crew for their work, being there for people when they most needed help. Dodger had great day where he met Patients whose lives were saved by the Air Ambulance and met the crew who work to save them. What a day!

The End!

Other books in the series:

How I Became Dodger Dog!

Dodger Dog's Muddy Mistake

Dodger Dog Meets Shea

Dodger Dog's Christmas Message

Dodger Dog at the Caravan

Dodger Dog Finds a Job

Dodger Dog Learns Something New

Dodger Dog say "No!" to Bullying

Dodger Dog loves the Oceans

Dodger Dog says Goodbye

Find out more about Dodger's mission to help others on his website: www.dodgerdog.co.uk

Also follow Dodger's antics on Twitter, Facebook & Instagram: @ I Love Dodger Dog

Join Dodger's free club on his website: "I love Dodger Dog club"

Printed in Great Britain
by Amazon